The King of the Polar Bears

and other magical stories

Compiled by Vic Parker

Miles Kelly

First published in 2012 by Miles Kelly Publishing Ltd
Harding's Barn, Bardfield End Green, Thaxted, Essex, CM6 3PX, UK

2 4 6 8 10 9 7 5 3 1

Publishing Director Belinda Gallagher
Creative Director Jo Cowan
Editorial Director Rosie McGuire
Editor Carly Blake
Senior Designer Joe Jones
Editorial Assistant Lauren White
Production Manager Elizabeth Collins
Reprographics Anthony Cambray, Stephan Davis, Jennifer Hunt

ISBN 978-1-84810-573-7

Printed in China

British Library Cataloguing-in-Publication Data
A catalogue record for this book is available from the British Library

ACKNOWLEDGEMENTS
The publishers would like to thank the following artists who have contributed to this book:
Cover: Peter Cottrill at The Bright Agency
Advocate Art: Alida Massari
The Bright Agency: Marcin Piwowarski, Tom Sperling
Marsela Hajdinjak

All other artwork from the Miles Kelly Artwork Bank

The publishers would like to thank the following sources for the use of their photographs:
Shutterstock: (page decorations) Dragana Francuski Tolimir
Dreamstime: (frames) Gordan

Every effort has been made to acknowledge the source and copyright holder of each picture.
Miles Kelly Publishing apologises for any unintentional errors or omissions.

Made with paper from a sustainable forest

www.mileskelly.net info@mileskelly.net

www.factsforprojects.com

Contents

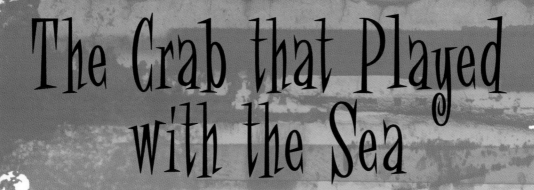

The Crab that Played with the Sea

From the *Just So* stories
by Rudyard Kipling

BEFORE THE HIGH and Far-Off Times, O my Best
Beloved, came the Time of the Very Beginnings,
and that was in the days when the Eldest Magician
was getting Things ready. First he got the Earth
ready, and then he got the Sea ready, and then he
told all the Animals that they could come out and
play. And the Animals said, "O Eldest Magician,
what shall we play at?"

And he said, "I will show you." He took the
Elephant and said, "Play at being an Elephant," and
the Elephant played. He took the Beaver and said,

"Play at being a Beaver," and the Beaver played. He took the Cow and said, "Play at being a Cow," and the Cow played. He took the Turtle and said, "Play at being a Turtle," and the Turtle played. One by one he took all the beasts and birds and fishes and told them what to play at.

Towards evening, there came up the Man, with his own best beloved little girl-daughter sitting upon his shoulder, and the Man said, "See that you make all the Animals obedient to me."

Now, while the Man and the Eldest Magician were talking together, Pau Amma the Crab, who was next in the game, scuttled off sideways and stepped into the sea, saying to himself, "I will play my play alone in the deep waters, and I will never be obedient to this son of Adam." Nobody saw him go away except the little girl-daughter.

And the play went on till there were no more Animals left without orders, and the Eldest Magician wiped the fine dust off his hands and walked about the world to see how the Animals were playing.

He went North, East, West and South, and by and by the Eldest Magician met the Man on the banks of the Perak river, and said, "Ho! Son of Adam, are all the Animals obedient to you?"

"Yes," said the Man.

"Is all the Earth obedient to you?"

"Yes," said the Man.

"Is all the Sea obedient to you?"

"No," said the Man. "Once a day and once a night the Sea runs up the Perak river and drives the sweet-water back into the forest, so that my house is made wet. Once a day and once a night it runs down the river and draws all the water after it, so that there is nothing left but mud, and my canoe is upset. Is that the play you told it to play?"

6

"No," said the Eldest Magician. "That is a new and a bad play. Launch your canoe and we will find out who is playing with the Sea."

They stepped into the canoe – the little girl-daughter came with them – and they pushed out on the Perak river and far out into the ocean. Then the Eldest Magician stood up and shouted, "Ho! Beasts, birds, and fishes, which one of you is playing with the Sea?"

Then all the beasts, birds, and fishes said together, "Eldest Magician, we play the plays that you taught us to play – we and our children's children. But not one of us plays with the Sea."

Then the little girl-daughter put up her little soft brown arms with the beautiful white shell bracelets and said, "O Eldest Magician! When my father here talked to you at the Very Beginning, one beast went away naughtily into the Sea before you had taught him his play. He was round and he was flat, and his eyes grew upon stalks, and he walked sideways like this, and he was covered with strong armour upon his back."

And the Eldest Magician said, "How wise are little children! Give me the paddle!"

So he took the paddle and paddled till they came to the place called Pusat Tasek – the Heart of the Sea. Then the Eldest Magician slid his arm up to the shoulder through the deep warm water, and touched the broad back of Pau Amma the Crab. Then the Eldest Magician called out, "What are you doing, Pau Amma?"

And Pau Amma, deep down below, answered, "Once a day and once a night I go out to look for my food. Once a day and once a night I return. Leave me alone."

Then the Eldest Magician said, "Listen, Pau Amma. When you go out from your cave

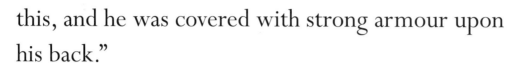

8

the waters of the Sea pour down into Pusat Tasek. When you come back and sit in Pusat Tasek, the waters of the Sea rise. If you are not afraid, come up and we will talk about it."

"I am not afraid," said Pau Amma, and he rose to the top of the sea, huge in the moonlight. No animal was as big as Pau Amma, for Pau Amma was King of all the crabs. "I didn't know I was so important," he said, rolling his eyes and waving his legs.

The Eldest Magician laughed. "You are not so important after all, Pau Amma," he said. And he made a Magic with just the little finger of his left hand – and lo and behold, Pau Amma's hard, rusty-copper-black shell fell off him as a husk falls off a coconut, and Pau Amma was left all soft.

Then Pau Amma said, "What shall I do? I am so enormous that I can only hide in Pusat Tasek, and if I go anywhere else, all soft as I am now, the sharks and the dogfish will eat me. And if I go to Pusat Tasek, all soft as I am now, though I may be safe, I can never stir out to get my food, and so I shall die." Then he waved his legs and lamented.

Then the Eldest Magician made a Magic with all five fingers of his right hand, and lo and behold, Best Beloved, Pau Amma grew smaller and smaller and smaller, till at last there was only a little coppery crab swimming in the water alongside the canoe.

And the girl-daughter took pity on him and gave him a pair of her scissors, and then Pau Amma was happier. He waved them in his little arms, and opened them and shut them and snapped them, and said, "I can eat nuts. I can crack shells. I can dig holes. I can climb trees. I can breathe in the dry air, and I can find a safe Pusat Tasek under every stone. I did not know I was so important!"

And the Eldest Magician said, "I will give you back your shell, Pau Amma, for eleven months of the year, but on the twelfth month of every year it shall grow soft again, to remind you and all your children that I can make magics, and to keep you humble, Pau Amma."

And from that day to this, you can see when you go to the beach, how all Pau Amma's babies make little Pusat Taseks for themselves under every stone and bunch of weed on the sands, and you can see them waving their little scissors. But once a year all Pau Ammas have to shake off their hard armour and be soft – to remind them of what the Eldest Magician could do.

The Butterfly that Stamped

From the *Just So* stories
by Rudyard Kipling

SULEIMAN-BIN-DAOUD was wise. He understood what the beasts said, what the birds said, what the fishes said, and what the insects said. He understood what the rocks said deep under the earth when they bowed in towards each other and groaned, and he understood what the trees said when they rustled in the morning.

Suleiman-bin-Daoud was strong. Upon the third finger of the right hand he wore a ring. When he turned it once, magical creatures called Djinns came out of the earth to do whatever he told them. When he turned it twice, Fairies came down from the sky to do whatever he told them. When he turned it three times, the very great angel Azrael of the Sword came and told him the news of the three worlds, Above – Below – and Here.

Suleiman-bin-Daoud married ever so many wives. He married nine hundred and ninety-nine wives, besides his Head Queen, the Most Beautiful Balkis. They all lived in a great golden palace in the middle of a lovely garden with fountains.

Some of the wives were nice, but some were simply horrid, and the horrid ones quarrelled with the nice ones and made them horrid too, and then they would all quarrel with Suleiman-bin-Daoud, and that was horrid for him. But Balkis the Most Beautiful never quarrelled with Suleiman-bin-Daoud. She loved him too much. She sat in her rooms in the Golden Palace, or walked in the Palace garden, and was truly sorry for him.

Whenever the nine hundred and ninety-nine

wives quarrelled too much, Suleiman-bin-Daoud walked by himself in one part of the beautiful Palace gardens. One day, when they had quarrelled for three weeks, Suleiman-bin-Daoud went out for peace and quiet, and among the orange trees he met Balkis the Most Beautiful, very sorrowful because Suleiman-bin-Daoud was so worried. And she said to him, "O my Lord and Light of my Eyes, turn the ring upon your finger and show these Queens of Egypt and Mesopotamia and Persia and China that you are the great and terrible King."

But Suleiman-bin-Daoud shook his head and said, "I must not use my power for the purpose of showing off. I shall continue to endure my fate."

So he went on between the lilies and the roses and the heavy-scented ginger-plants that grew in the garden, till he came to a great camphor-tree. But Balkis hid among the tall irises and the spotted bamboos behind the camphor-tree, so as to be near her own true love.

14

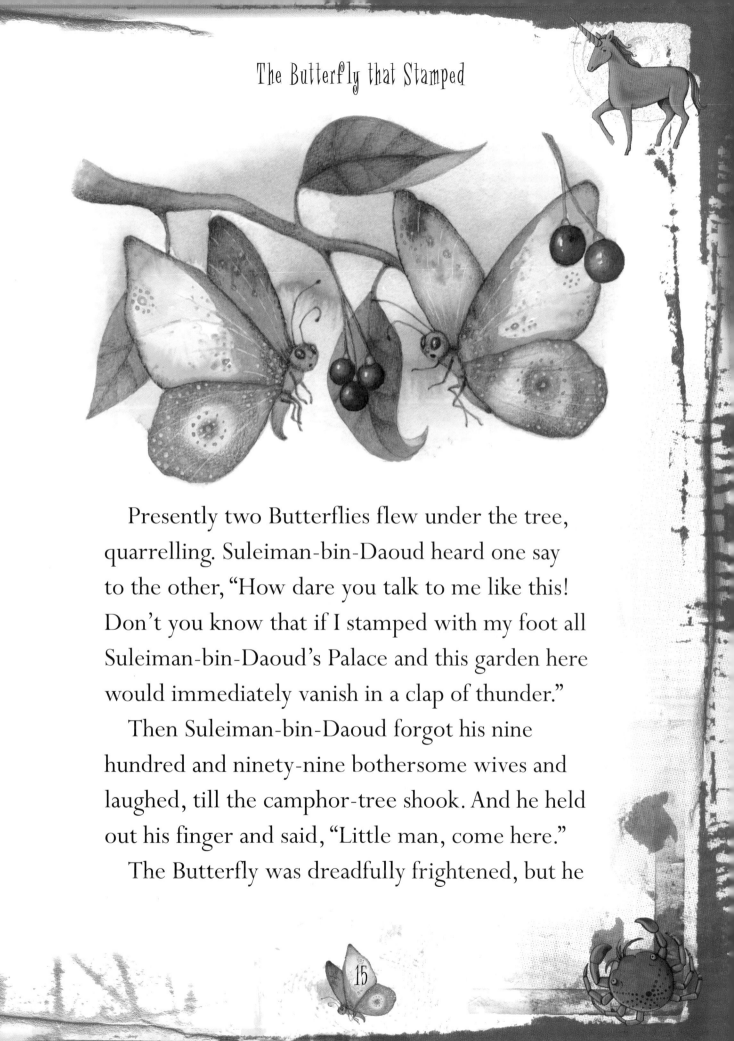

Presently two Butterflies flew under the tree, quarrelling. Suleiman-bin-Daoud heard one say to the other, "How dare you talk to me like this! Don't you know that if I stamped with my foot all Suleiman-bin-Daoud's Palace and this garden here would immediately vanish in a clap of thunder."

Then Suleiman-bin-Daoud forgot his nine hundred and ninety-nine bothersome wives and laughed, till the camphor-tree shook. And he held out his finger and said, "Little man, come here."

The Butterfly was dreadfully frightened, but he

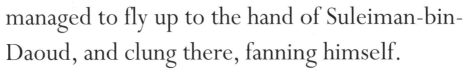

managed to fly up to the hand of Suleiman-bin-Daoud, and clung there, fanning himself.

Suleiman-bin-Daoud bent his head and whispered very softly, "Little man, what made you tell that awful fib to your wife? For doubtless she is your wife."

The Butterfly picked up his courage and said, "O King, you know what wives are like. She has been quarrelling with me all the morning. I said that to quiet her."

And Suleiman-bin-Daoud said, "May it quiet her. Go back to your wife, little brother, and let me hear what you say."

Back flew the Butterfly to his wife, who was all of a twitter behind a leaf, and she said, "And what did he say? Oh, what did he say?"

"Well," said the Butterfly, fanning himself most importantly, "between you and me, my dear, he asked me not to stamp, and I promised I wouldn't."

"Gracious!" said his wife, and sat quite quiet, but

Suleiman-bin-Daoud laughed till the tears ran down his face at the impudence of the bad little Butterfly.

Balkis the Most Beautiful stood up behind the tree and smiled to herself, for she had heard all this talk. She thought, 'Maybe I can yet save my Lord from these quarrelsome Queens,' and she held out her finger and whispered softly to the Butterfly's Wife, "Little woman, come here." Up flew the Butterfly's Wife, very frightened, and clung to Balkis's white hand. Balkis bent her beautiful head down and whispered, "Little woman, do you believe what your husband has just said?"

The Butterfly's Wife picked up her courage and said, "O Queen, you know what men-folk are like. They get angry over nothing at all and they never mean half they say. If it pleases my husband to believe that I believe he can make Suleiman-bin-Daoud's Palace disappear by stamping his foot, I'm sure I don't care. He'll forget all about it tomorrow."

"Little sister," said Balkis, "you are quite right, but next time he begins to boast, take him at his word. Ask him to stamp, and see what will happen. He'll be very much ashamed."

Away flew the Butterfly's Wife to her husband, and in five minutes they were quarrelling worse than ever.

"Remember!" said the Butterfly. "Remember what I can do if I stamp my foot."

"I dare you to do it," said his wife. "Stamp! Stamp! Stamp!"

The Butterfly, very hot and puffy, came whirling back to the King and said, "She wants me to stamp! You know nothing will happen, and she'll never again believe a word I say!"

"No, little brother," said Suleiman-bin-Daoud, who was laughing most joyously. And he turned the ring on his finger and, lo and behold, four huge Djinns came out of the earth!

"Slaves," said Suleiman-bin-Daoud, "when this

gentleman on my finger stamps his left front forefoot you will make my Palace and these gardens disappear in a clap of thunder. When he stamps again you will bring them back carefully."

Away flew the Butterfly to his wife, who was crying, "I dare you to do it! Stamp now!"

Balkis saw the four vast Djinns stoop down to the four corners of the gardens with the Palace in the middle, and she clapped her hands softly and said, "At last Suleiman-bin-Daoud will do for the sake of a Butterfly what he ought to have done long ago for his own sake, and the quarrelsome Queens will be frightened!"

The butterfly stamped. The Djinns jerked the Palace and the gardens a thousand miles into the air, there was a most awful thunder-clap, and everything grew inky-black.

The Butterfly was nearly as frightened as his wife, and Suleiman-bin-Daoud laughed so much that it was several minutes before he found breath enough

to whisper to the Butterfly, "Stamp again, most great magician."

So he stamped once more, and that instant the Djinns let down the Palace and the gardens, without even a bump.

The Butterfly's Wife lay on her side under the camphor-tree waggling her wings and panting, "Oh, I'll be good! I'll be good!"

Suleiman-bin-Daoud could hardly speak for laughing.

Then came a terrible noise. All the nine hundred and ninety-nine Queens ran out of the Palace shrieking. They hurried down the great marble steps below the fountain, one hundred abreast, and the Most Wise Balkis went forward to meet them and said, "What is your trouble, O Queens?"

They stood on the marble steps one hundred abreast and shouted, "Suddenly our Palace disappeared, and we were left sitting in a thick and noisome darkness!"

Then Balkis said, "It is nothing, O Queens! A Butterfly has made complaint against his wife because she quarrelled with him, and it has pleased our Lord Suleiman-bin-Daoud to teach her a lesson. Come and see."

The Queens ran down the steps, and beneath his camphor-tree, still weak with laughing, they saw the Most Wise King Suleiman-bin-Daoud rocking back and forth with a Butterfly on either hand.

21

Then all the Queens except Balkis fell flat on their faces, for they said, "If these things are done when a Butterfly is displeased with his wife, what shall be done to us who have vexed our King with our loud-speaking and open quarrelling through many days?"

Then they put their veils over their heads, and they all went up to the Palace and lived happily ever afterwards – including Suleiman-bin-Daoud and his equally wise wife, Balkis.

The King of the Polar Bears

From *American Fairy Tales*
by L Frank Baum

THE KING of the Polar Bears lived among the icebergs in the deep cold of the far north country. He was old, monstrous big, and very wise. His body was thickly covered with long, white hair that glistened silver under the midnight sun. His claws were strong and sharp, that he might walk over the smooth ice or grasp and tear the fishes and seals upon which he fed.

The seals were afraid of him, but the gulls – both white and grey – loved him because he left the remnants of his feasts for them.

Often his subjects, the polar bears, came to him for advice when they were ill or in trouble, but they kept away from his hunting grounds, lest they might arouse his anger.

The wolves, who sometimes came as far north as the icebergs, whispered among themselves that the King of the Polar Bears was a magician. For no earthly thing seemed able to harm him – he never failed to secure plenty of food, and he grew bigger and stronger day by day.

Yet the time came when this monarch of the north met man, and his wisdom failed him.

He came out of his cave among the icebergs one day and saw a boat moving through a strip of water uncovered by the shifting of the summer ice. In the boat were men.

The great bear had never seen such creatures before, and advanced sniffing the strange scent with aroused curiosity.

When the king came near the water's edge a man

stood up in the boat and with a queer instrument made a loud 'Bang!' The polar bear felt a shock, his brain became numb, his thoughts deserted him, his great limbs shook and gave way beneath him and his body fell heavily upon the hard ice.

That was all he remembered for a time.

When he awoke he was smarting with pain on every inch of his huge bulk, for the men had cut away his hide with its glorious white hair and carried it with them to a distant ship.

Above him circled thousands of his friends, the gulls, wondering if their benefactor were really dead and it was proper to eat him. But when they saw him raise his head and groan and tremble they knew he still lived, and one of them said to his comrades: "The wolves were right. The king is a great magician, for even men cannot kill him. But he suffers greatly for lack of covering. Let us repay his kindness to us by each giving him as many feathers as we can spare."

One after another they plucked with their beaks the softest feathers from under their wings, and, flying down, dropped them gently upon his body.

Then they called to him in a chorus: "Our feathers are as soft and beautiful as your own shaggy hair. They will guard you from the cold winds and warm you while you sleep."

And the King of the Polar Bears had courage to bear his pain and lived and was strong again.

The rest of that summer and all through the six months of night the king left his icy cavern only to fish or catch seals for food. He felt no shame at his feathery covering, but it was still strange to him, and he avoided meeting any of his brother bears.

26

When the moon fell away from the sky and the sun came to make the icebergs glitter with the gorgeous tintings of the rainbow, two of the polar bears arrived at the king's cavern to ask his advice about the hunting season. But when they saw his great body covered with feathers instead of hair they began to laugh, and one said: "Our mighty king has become a bird! Who ever before heard of a feathered polar bear?"

Then the king gave way to wrath. He advanced upon them with deep growls and stately tread and with one blow of his monstrous paw stretched the mocker lifeless at his feet.

The other ran away to his fellows and carried the news of the king's strange appearance. The result was a meeting of all the polar bears upon a broad field of ice, where they talked gravely of the remarkable change that had come upon their monarch.

"He is, in reality, no longer a bear," said one, "nor

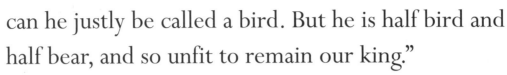

can he justly be called a bird. But he is half bird and half bear, and so unfit to remain our king."

"I will fight him," growled a particularly huge bear. "I – Woof – the strongest of our race! I will be King of the Polar Bears instead."

The others nodded agreement, and dispatched a messenger to the king to say he must fight the great Woof and beat him, if he would stay ruler.

When the king heard this he visited his friends, the gulls, and told them of the coming battle. "I shall conquer," he said, proudly. "Yet my people are in the right, for only a hairy one like themselves can hope to command their obedience."

The queen gull said: "I met an eagle yesterday, who had flown over a big city of men. The eagle told me he had seen a monstrous polar bear skin thrown over the back of a carriage that rolled along the street. That skin must have been yours, oh king, and if you wish I will send one hundred of my gulls to the city to bring it back to you."

"Let them go!" said the king, gruffly. And the hundred gulls were soon flying rapidly southward.

For three days they flew straight as an arrow, until they came to scattered houses, to villages, and to cities. Then their search began.

The gulls were brave, cunning and wise. Upon the fourth day they reached the great metropolis, and hovered over the streets until a carriage rolled along with a great white bear robe thrown over the back seat. Then the birds swooped down and, seizing the skin in their beaks, flew quickly away.

They were late. The king's great battle was upon the seventh day, and they must fly swiftly to reach the Polar regions by that time.

Meanwhile the bird-bear was preparing for his fight. He sharpened his claws in the small crevasses of the ice. He caught a seal and tested his big yellow teeth by crunching its bones between them. And the queen gull set her band to pluming the king bear's feathers until they lay smoothly upon his body.

But every day they cast anxious glances into the southern sky, watching for the hundred gulls to bring back the king's own skin.

The seventh day came, and all the polar bears in that region gathered around the king's cavern. Among them was Woof, confident of his success.

"The bird-bear's feathers will fly fast enough when I get my claws upon him!" he boasted, and the others laughed and encouraged him.

The king was sad at not having recovered his skin, but he resolved to fight bravely without it. He

30

advanced from his cavern with a kingly bearing, and when he faced his enemy he gave so terrible a growl that Woof's heart stopped beating for a moment, and he began to realise that a fight with the wise and mighty king of his race was no laughing matter.

After exchanging a few heavy blows with his foe Woof's courage returned, and he decided to dishearten his adversary by bluster.

"Come nearer, bird-bear!" he cried, "So that I may pluck your plumage!"

Filled with rage, the king ruffled his feathers till he seemed to be twice his actual size. He struck Woof a blow which cracked his skull like an egg-shell and he fell prone upon the ground.

While the assembled bears stood looking with fear and wonder at their fallen champion the sky became darkened.

One hundred gulls flew down from above and dropped upon the king's body a skin covered with pure white hair that glittered in the sun like silver.

And behold! The bears saw before them the well-known form of their wise and respected master, and with one accord they bowed their shaggy heads in homage to the mighty King of the Polar Bears.

The Egg

An extract from *The Phoenix and the Carpet*
by E Nesbit

Five children — Cyril, Anthea, Robert, Jane, and the youngest, 'the Lamb',
are in their playroom. Their mother recently bought a new carpet for the room.
It was delivered rolled up, and when the children laid it out, they found inside
a strange golden egg, which they have placed on the mantelpiece…

I WISH they taught magic at school," Jane sighed. "I believe if we could do a little magic it might make something happen."

"I wonder how you begin?" Robert looked round the room, but he got no ideas from the faded green curtains, or the drab Venetian blinds, or the worn brown oil-cloth on the floor. Even the new carpet suggested nothing, though its pattern was a very wonderful one, and always seemed as though it were

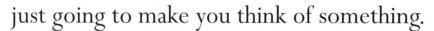

just going to make you think of something.

"I could begin right enough," said Anthea, "I've read about it. But I believe it's wrong in the Bible."

"It's only wrong in the Bible because people might use it to hurt other people. We don't want to hurt anybody, and what's more, we jolly well couldn't if we tried. Let's get the *Ingoldsby Legends*. There's a thing about Abra-cadabra there," said Cyril, yawning.

"I'll get *Ingoldsby*," said Anthea. "You turn up the hearthrug."

So they traced strange figures on the linoleum, where the hearthrug had kept it clean. They traced them with chalk that Robert had nicked from the top of the mathematical master's desk at school. And they chanted all the gloomiest songs they could think of. And, of course, nothing happened.

So then Anthea said, "I'm sure a magic fire ought to be made of sweet-smelling wood, and have magic gums and essences and things in it."

"I don't know any sweet-smelling wood, except

34

cedar," said Robert, "but I've got some ends of cedar-wood lead pencil."

So they burned the ends of lead pencil. And still nothing happened.

"Let's burn some of the eucalyptus oil we have for our colds," said Anthea.

And they did. It certainly smelled very strong. And they burned lumps of camphor out of the big chest. It was very bright, and made lots of horrid black smoke, which looked very magical indeed. But still nothing happened. Then they got some clean tea-cloths from the dresser drawer in the kitchen, and waved them over the magic chalk-tracings, and sang 'The Hymn of the Moravian Nuns at Bethlehem', which is very impressive. And still nothing happened. So they waved more and more wildly, and then Robert's tea-cloth accidentally caught the golden egg and whisked it off the mantelpiece, and it fell into the fender and rolled under the grate.

"Oh, crikey!" said more than one voice.

And everyone instantly fell down flat on their fronts to look under the grate, and there lay the egg, glowing in a nest of hot ashes.

"It's not smashed, anyhow," said Robert, and he put his hand under the grate and picked up the egg. But the egg was much hotter than anyone would have believed it could possibly get in such a short time, and Robert had to drop it with a cry of "Bother!" It fell on the top bar of the grate, and then bounced right into the glowing red-hot heart of the fire.

"The tongs!" cried Anthea. But, alas, no one could remember where they were. Everyone had forgotten that the tongs had last been used to fish up the doll's teapot from the bottom of the water-butt, where the Lamb had dropped it. So the nursery tongs were resting between the water-butt and the dustbin.

"Never mind," said Robert, "we'll get it out with the poker and the shovel."

"Oh, stop," cried Anthea. "Look at it! Quick, look! Look! Look! I do believe something IS going to happen!"

For the egg was now red-hot, and inside it something was moving. Next moment there was a soft cracking sound, the egg burst in two, and out of it came a flame-coloured bird.

It rested a
moment among
the flames, and as
it rested there the
four children could
see it growing bigger and
bigger under their eyes.

Every mouth was a-gape,
every eye a-goggle.

The bird rose in its nest of
fire, stretched its wings, and flew
out into the room. It flew round and
round, and then round again, and where it
passed the air was warm. Then it perched on the
fender. The children looked at each other. Then
Cyril put out a hand towards the bird. It put
its head on one side and looked up at him,
just as you may have seen a parrot do when
it is getting ready to speak, so that the
children were hardly astonished

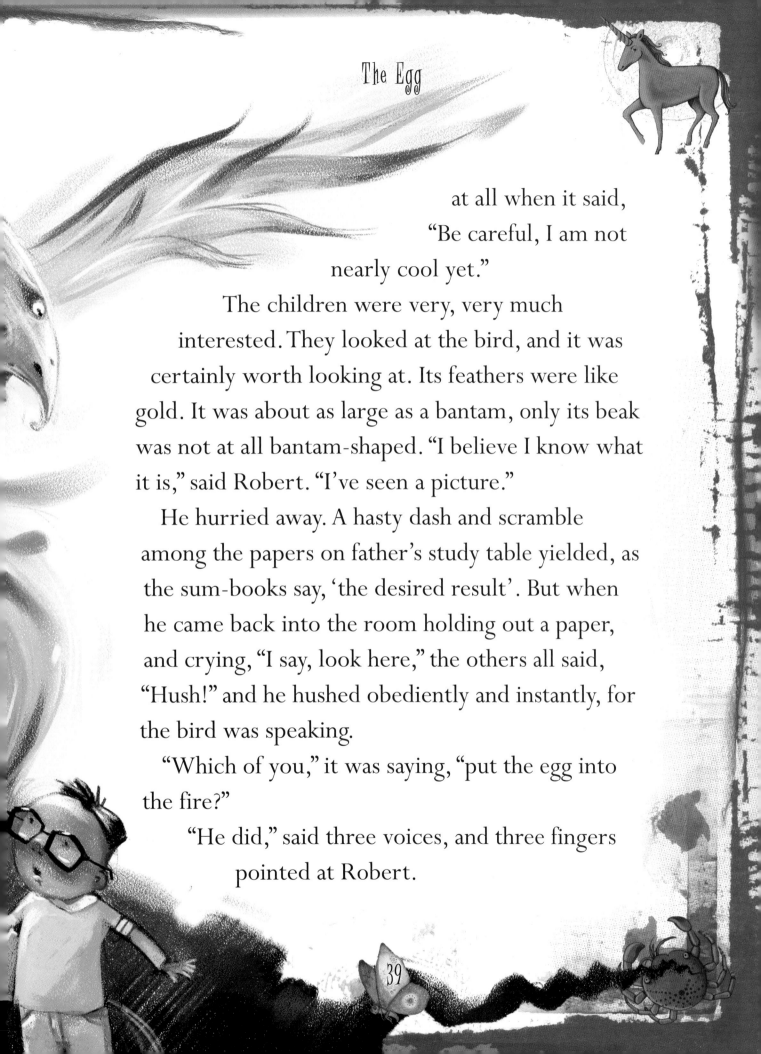

at all when it said, "Be careful, I am not nearly cool yet."

The children were very, very much interested. They looked at the bird, and it was certainly worth looking at. Its feathers were like gold. It was about as large as a bantam, only its beak was not at all bantam-shaped. "I believe I know what it is," said Robert. "I've seen a picture."

He hurried away. A hasty dash and scramble among the papers on father's study table yielded, as the sum-books say, 'the desired result'. But when he came back into the room holding out a paper, and crying, "I say, look here," the others all said, "Hush!" and he hushed obediently and instantly, for the bird was speaking.

"Which of you," it was saying, "put the egg into the fire?"

"He did," said three voices, and three fingers pointed at Robert.

39

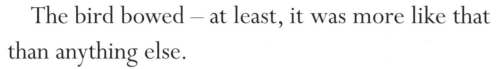

The bird bowed – at least, it was more like that than anything else.

"I am your grateful debtor," it said with a high-bred air.

The children were all choking with wonder and curiosity – all except Robert. He held the paper in his hand, and he KNEW. He said so. He said:

"I know who you are."

And he opened and displayed a printed paper, at the head of which was a little picture of a bird sitting in a nest of flames.

"You are the Phoenix," said Robert, and the bird was quite pleased.